To all the working mothers who show their love in countless and immeasurable ways every day.

And I Thought About You…

Rosanne L. Kurstedt

Illustrated by Lisa Carletta-Vieites

Nestled in a great big hug, you whisper in my ear, "What did you do today, Mama?"

I woke up early. Got ready for work.

Made coffee. And I thought about you…

…sleeping peacefully in your bed. Hugging your stuffed puppy and dreaming of bouncy balls and butterflies.

I sat in traffic. Heard horns honking.

Worried I'd be late. And I thought about you…

...scooping your milk-soaked cereal with your favorite purple spoon.

I arrived at my office. Stepped into the shiny-mirrored elevator. Pushed the button to the 17th floor.

And I thought about you...

Ding

Ding

...wrinkling your forehead as you dress yourself.

First your pants, one leg at a time. Then your shirt, making sure you put your head through the right hole.

I turned on the computer. Answered e-mails from customers and co-workers. Wrote important letters. And I thought about you…

Clickity-Clack

Clickity-Clack

...learning to say your ABCs and drawing one-of-a-kind designs, using all the colors in the rainbow.

I went to a meeting. Sat at a l-o-o-o-ng mahogany table. Planned a business trip. And I thought about you…

…playing airplane in the park with your arms spread wide. Running as fast as you can before circling and slowing down for a landing.

Chit. Chat. Splat.

I ate lunch with my friends. Had a slice of pizza.

The sauce splattered on my shirt.

And I thought about you...

...eating a grilled cheese sandwich, trying to see how long you could stretch the cheese before the gooey threads stick to your chin.

Rrrring
Rrrrring

I went back to my office. Dialed the telephone.

Spoke to Daddy. And we thought about you…

...laughing with joy
as you and your friends create
the biggest, bestest zoo ever –
where lions and leopards wander
freely alongside dinosaurs and dolphins.

Shuffle. Swish.

I cleaned my desk and got ready to go home.
Stacked piles of paper as high as skyscrapers.
And I thought about you...

...sitting quietly
on Nana's lap,
reading through
a pile of your
favorite books.

I stopped at the store. Bought a special treat.
And I thought about you…

…standing on tiptoes as you reach to set the table. Napkins first, then the spoons, and finally the forks. Making sure everything is perfectly straight.

Mama... Daddy... Nana... Me...

Ding

Dong

When I got to our house, I rang the bell. I know how you love to meet me at the door.

I heard the sound of your running feet and the sound of your sing-song voice, "Who's there?"

"It's me, Mama." I answered playfully.

I opened the door and saw your joyful face brighten.

"Mama, Mama," you sang out.

I bent down, swaddled you in my arms, and whispered in your ear, "What did you do today?"

Excitedly you answered, "I went to the park, ate grilled cheese, played zoo with my friends –

and...

... I thought about you."

Rosanne Kurstedt

And I Thought About You grew out of a bedtime routine Rosanne and her first son invented when their family lived in Hong Kong. The routine crossed the Pacific Ocean when she and her family returned to the United States, and lives on in their hearts to this day. Her love of picture books and passion for sharing wonderfully crafted stories drew her to capture the "And I Thought About You" routine into a book. A former teacher, Rosanne is currently an Adjunct Professor of Education at Fordham University. She is the author of a professional book for teachers entitled *Teaching Writing with Picture Books as Models*, which was published by Scholastic in 2000. She lives in New Jersey with her two boys, husband, and dog Dorothy.

Lisa Carletta-Vieites

As a working mother of three daughters, Lisa can relate to this book's poignant message. She is an Associate Director in the financial industry, and in her spare time she pursues her life-long hobby of art and drawing. As such, this is her first foray into picture book illustrating. She lives in New Jersey with her husband, kids, and two dogs.